For Nana and Baba,
for Scrabble and stories

ISBN 978-0-06-291605-1

The artist used acrylic, gouache, colored pencil, crayon, and Photoshop
to create the illustrations for this book.
Typography by Dana Fritts
20 21 22 23 24 RTLO 10 9 8 7 6 5 4 3 2 1 ❖ First Edition

THESAURUS HAS A SECRET

Written and illustrated by
ANYA GLAZER

KT KATHERINE TEGEN BOOKS
An Imprint of HarperCollins Publishers

Millions of years ago, dinosaurs ruled the world. There were fearsome T. rexes, nimble Iguanodons, and great-horned Triceratopses.

But this isn't a story about them.
This is a story about . . .

Thesaurus.

Thesaurus was just like other dinosaurs . . .

mostly.

He ate, like other dinosaurs . . .

and played, like other dinosaurs. . . .

Whatever other dinosaurs did, Thesaurus did too.

Whether it was arm wrestling

or ball games,

he did it all, just with a wider vocabulary.

But Thesaurus also had a secret.

Something he loved more than words.

When no one was looking, he loved to . . .

read.

Jurassic Mansfield Park

STEGOSAURUS AND SENSIBILITY

The Mill on the Fossil

A BRIEF HISTORY OF THE LAND BEFORE TIME

THE LOST WORLD

LOVE IN THE METEORS

The Phantom Tollbooth

Moby Diplodocus

A Tail of Two Cities

To Kill a M

ONE FLEW OVER THE PTERODACTYL'S NEST

The Tyrannosaurus Who Came to Tea

Littl

OEDIPUS T. REX

Five Children and Ichthyosaur

WHERE THE WILD THINGS A

THE BROTHERS CAMARASAURU

PARADISE LOST

Cretaceous Expectations

We'r Bront

OF MICRORAPTORS AND MEN

The Adventures of Saurolophus Holmes

The Secret Gar

The Amber Sp

PTEROSAUR P

ONE HUNDRED AND FIFTY MILLION YEARS OF SOLITUDE

ANKYLOSAURUS OF GREEN GABLES

ALBERTOSAURUS CAMUS

The T.

T. REX OF THE D'URBERVILLES

witc

d Prejud

MIDDLEM

THE STRANGER

THE STRANGER

ALLOSAURUS'S ADVENTURES IN WONDERLAND

JANE EYRE

JANE EYRE

CHARLOTTE BRONTËSAURUS

He would read anytime

and anywhere.

All he needed was a comfy spot . . .
nice and hidden from view.

If anyone ever came close, Thesaurus
was always ready with an excuse.

No one could ever discover his secret.
Reading just wasn't something dinosaurs did.

Sometimes he wished he could share his
love of stories with someone.

But in the company of a good book, he never really felt alone.

He would get
swept up in
the magic,

lose himself in new worlds,

stars

mystery and wonder

journey with friends,

and have grand adventures.

and then all of a sudden

One day, he'd been so absorbed that he hadn't even realized he was reading out loud.

Maybe no one had noticed.

(Maybe they had.)

Oh no.

Disaster. Bad.

What had he done? How would he ever fit in now? Thesaurus had never felt more terrified or alone.

Already the others were starting to make fun of him; one of them kept poking his tail. . . .

Thesaurus loved to read. More than that—
He savored each sentence. He relished the words.

He treasured

and cherished

and adored

and delighted

in every single story.

And, as it turned out . . .

Everyone else loved to listen.